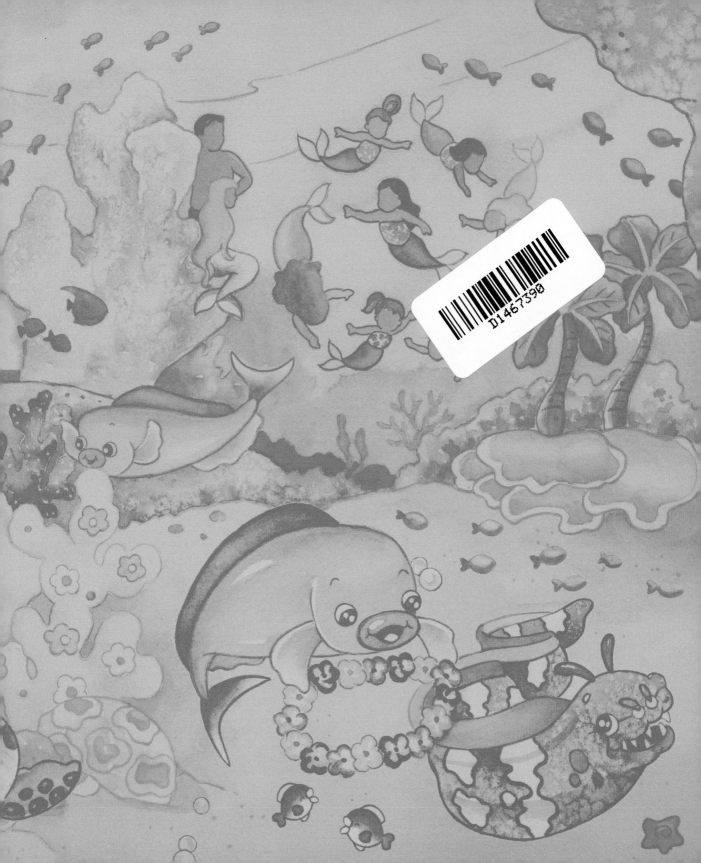

Momi

A Hawaiian Mermaid
in the Land of Delight

Written by Elaine Masters

Illustrated by Yuko Green

Published and distributed by

ISLAND HERITAGE
P U B L I S H I N G
94-411 KŌʻAKI STREET, WAIPAHU, HAWAIʻI 96797
PHONE: (800) 468-2800 • FAX: (808) 488-2279
WEBSITE: www.islandheritage.com

ISBN# : 0-89610-356-0

First Edition, First Printing - 2001

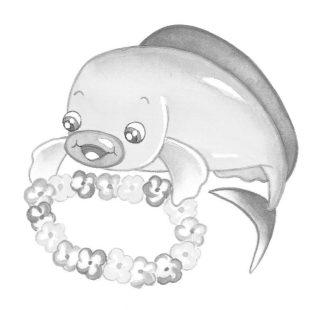

DEDICATION

To David, Vickie, Jennifer and Kevin,
who swam like mermaids
even when they were small,
Elaine Masters

To Annie and Katherine,
Yuko Green

Once upon a time,
Deep in the Pacific Ocean—
deeper than you can imagine—
a little mermaid lived with her
family in a coral house.
The mermaid's name was Momi.

One day, Momi and her best friend, Manny the Mahimahi, were swimming around in circles. Their neighbor, gruff old Elsie the Eel, came writhing by.

"I'm bored," Momi told Elsie the Eel. "There's nothing to do around here. I want to have some fun."

She tossed her head and wiggled her tail. (She always did that when she felt impatient.)

7

"Follow me," said Elsie the Eel.
"I'll take you to a special Land of Delight."

Elsie the Eel swam away,
and Momi the Mermaid and
Manny the Mahimahi followed behind.

Soon they met Cheeky the Turtle.

"Where are you going?"
asked Cheeky.
"We're going to the
Land of Delight," said
Momi. "We're going to have
some wonderful fun."

"May I go with you?" asked Cheeky.
"Of course," said Momi.

And off they swam,
Elsie the Eel,
and Momi the Mermaid,
Cheeky the Turtle,
and at the end, Momi's very best friend,
Manny the Mahimahi.

Soon they met Wiki the Whale.

"Where are you going?" asked Wiki.

"We're going to the Land of Delight," said Momi.

"We're going to have some awesome fun."

"May I go with you?" asked Wiki.

"Of course," said Momi.

12

And off they swam,
Elsie the Eel,
and Momi the Mermaid,
Cheeky the Turtle,
and Wiki the Whale,
and at the end,
Momi's very best friend,
Manny the Mahimahi.

Soon they met Dandi the Dolphin.

"Where are you going?" asked Dandi.

"We're going to the Land of Delight," said Momi.

"We're going to have some marvelous fun."

"May I go with you?" asked Dandi.

"Of course," said Momi.

And off they swam,
Elsie the Eel,
and Momi the Mermaid,
Cheeky the Turtle,
and Wiki the Whale,
Dandi the Dolphin,
and at the end,
Momi's very
best friend,
Manny the
Mahimahi.

Soon they met Moki the Monk Seal.

"Where are you going?" asked Moki.
"We're going to the Land of Delight," said Momi.
"We're going to have some incredible fun."
"May I go with you?" asked Moki.
"Of course," said Momi.

And off they swam,
   Elsie the Eel,
    and Momi the Mermaid,
      Cheeky the Turtle,
        and Wiki the Whale,
          Dandi the Dolphin,
            and Moki the Monk Seal,
              and way at the end,
                Momi's very best friend, Manny the Mahimahi.

"Are we there yet?"
asked Momi.

"Almost,"
said gruff
old Elsie
the Eel.

17

They swam around a big coral reef, Elsie and all the rest. The rocks looked suspiciously familiar to Momi, and she began to wiggle her tail. (She always did that when she felt impatient.)

"Here we are," said Elsie the Eel.

"But you brought us right back home," said Momi, wiggling her tail extra hard. "This isn't the Land of Delight."

"Of course it is," said Elsie. "You just have to make it so."

"What do you mean?" asked Momi. "It's boring here, and we wanted to have some wonderful, awesome, marvelous, incredible fun."

"Just hold your tail still and listen, Momi."

Then Elsie the Eel explained, "Each one of you has a talent. You can teach the rest of us how to do the special thing that only you can do. It will be awesome and wonderful, I promise. You'll be delighted. Just you wait and see. We'll start with Cheeky. What can you do?"

"I can push like a sumo wrestler," said Cheeky.

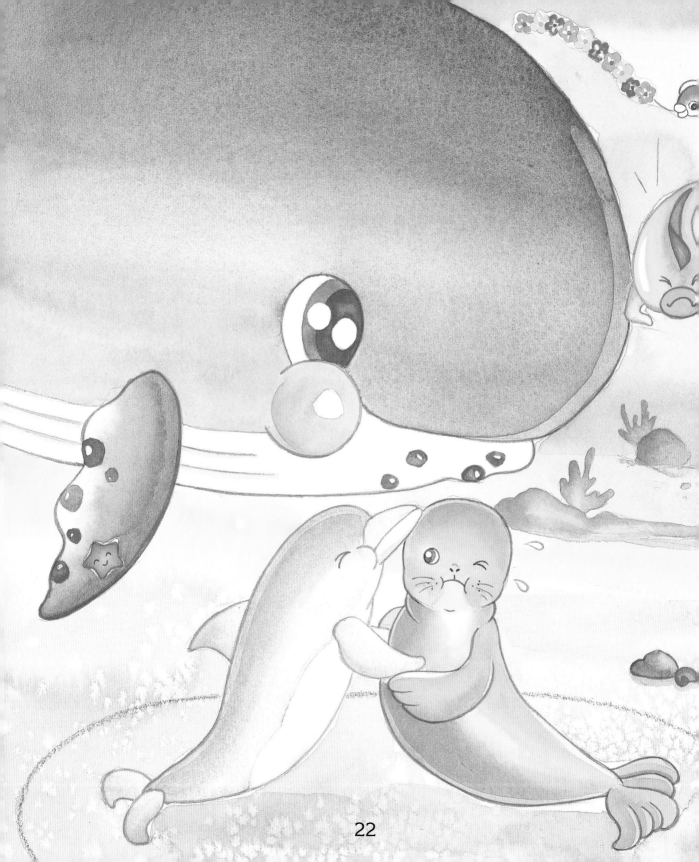

"That's great!" said Elsie the Eel.
"All right, everybody. Pair off."

And everyone paired off to push each
other. They pushed and pushed. They fell
down and got up and pushed some more.
Soon they were laughing. "This really IS fun," said Momi.

"Of course," said Elsie. "What did I tell you?
And now, who is next?"

23

Wiki the Whale could spout water like a fountain.

Dandi the Dolphin could leap over the waves.

Moki the Monk Seal could twist and turn and wave his flipper.

Everyone looked so funny, trying to imitate the special thing that only one of them could do. Everyone laughed and laughed. Everyone, that is, but Manny.

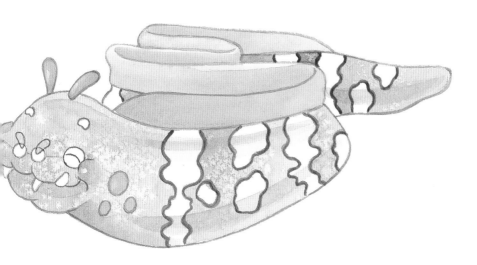

The little Mahimahi hung his big blunt head and looked sad. "I can't do anything special," he said. "All I can do is swim, and that's something all of you already can do."

Momi put her arms around Manny. "Oh, Manny, you do know how to do something special. You know how to be a friend!"

Momi turned to gruff old Elsie the Eel and smiled. "You really did know best.

I see now how it operates.

When everyone cooperates—

My home becomes a wonderful Land of Delight."

And then,

Momi the Mermaid,

and Cheeky the Turtle,

Wiki the Whale,

and Dandi the Dolphin,

Moki the Monk Seal

and Manny the Mahimahi said,

"Three cheers for Elsie the Eel! She had the best idea ever!"

Elsie the Eel coughed and tried to put on a gruff face.

But when Momi looked close, she saw a twinkle in the old eel's eye.

Elsie was so-o-o pleased!

THE END